Highboy Rings Down the Curtain

Highboy Rings Down the Curtain

By

GEORGE AGNEW CHAMBERLAIN

2023

Highboy Rings Down the Curtain

FIRST FOREWORD.

When I was a young child, I was lifted onto a horse as a second rider. I had a great fear of heights and an even greater fear of the gigantic animal I found myself clinging to for dear life. No hippophile, I. The horse took off on what was probably just a trot or slow canter, but it appeared to me that I was about to meet my end. I survived, of course, though it seemed a near thing. Years later, a cousin invited me to spend some time at her horse ranch. Although I was still afraid of horses, I had grown to admire their great beauty, so I agreed. What I found during my time there was truly enlightening. Not only are horses impressive in their strength and beauty, but they are also extremely loyal and intelligent creatures.

It had rained the night before we were supposed to go to the paddocks, and since spring rains in Alabama involve orange, slippery, muddy clay, we both donned rubber boots before heading out. To my amazement, my cousin walked right into the midst of many tons of two-year-old fillies as if they were puppies. Upon her advice of "Don't look scared, they'll know," I followed her on in, trusty camera around my neck. What a magical experience! They walked right up to me, friendly and curious, to see who this new person was in their space and whether my camera tasted like apples. One of them looked me right in the eye and I could have sworn she was taking my measure and if she could have, she would have gently and reassuringly asked me my name. Such intelligence and emotion in her expression; it was so unexpected, and I will never forget that day. I came away with a new understanding of the nature of horses.

Still, upon hearing that this book is a story about a man and his horse, one might be tempted to think, "Oh, another one of those," as I did. After reading it, though, I found that I had gained an entirely different perspective. Initially, the story seems to be the tale of a gentleman named Kindly Crewe, affectionately nicknamed so due to his sweet and kind nature, and to the way he grieved over the loss of his beloved horse, Helen of Troy. The story tells us how much he adored Helen of Troy and how terribly he mourned her loss. But it also tells the tale of those around Kindly who cared deeply about him. It tells how they banded together to support him in his grief and ultimately helped him regain joy in his life.

The remainder of the story pivots around a high-spirited gelding named Highboy, who had been given up as too recalcitrant to ever be a show horse. Bimbo, Kindly's resident horse trainer, believed that Highboy had great potential and needed someone like Kindly to give him a reason to show off his abilities. The story goes on to tell us just how that happens.

After I finished reading *Highboy*, I was reminded of my experiences at my cousin's ranch that day and how it changed my whole outlook about these remarkable animals. After you finish reading the story, I invite you to consider what the ending reveals about horses and how it compares to your own view of these surprising, marvelous giants.

Randi Ward

George Agnew Chamberlain

SECOND FOREWORD.

George Agnew Chamberlain, who wrote *Highboy Rings Down the Curtain*, is a largely forgotten South Jersey author who lived and wrote during the twentieth century. From the 1920s to the 1960s, he resided in Salem County, New Jersey. In 1927, Chamberlain purchased Lloyd's Landing on the Alloways Creek. From there he researched and wrote about the people and places he came to love in what Chamberlain called the Barrens. He died in 1966.

Though not originally from New Jersey—he was born in San Paulo, Brazil, in 1879, the child of missionaries—he came to America in 1891 to continue his education. As a young adult he graduated from Lawrenceville School in Mercer County, New Jersey, and went on to attend Princeton for two years.

In 1902, he returned to Brazil to teach, sell religious books, and, finally, join the consular service. It was also at this time that he began to write and have his stories published. He came back to America for a short time and then returned to Brazil as the Consul General in Pernambuco. From Brazil he was assigned to Lourenco Marques in Portuguese East Africa and from there to Mexico City, Mexico. He resigned from the service in 1919 to write full time.

Highboy Rings Down the Curtain is Chamberlain's first story based in South Jersey. It was published in the *Saturday Evening Post* in December 1922 and then republished, in expanded form, by the *Bridgeton Evening News* in a limited edition of 300 copies. Though short in length, it was featured in *The Sporting Spirit: An Anthology* (1925), *Hosses: An Anthology of Short Stories* (1937), *New Stories for Men* (1941 and 1943), and *Great Horse Stories* (1946).

This new edition of *Highboy Rings Down The Curtain* is based upon a copy of the first edition donated by William W. Leap and preserved in the Bjork Library Special Collections at Stockton University. The editing and design team for this 100th-anniversary commemorative edition include Kyle Annassenz, Anthony Bastos, Zophia Krause, Gabrielle Shockley, Sheisa Tapia, Randi Ward and Tom Kinsella.

CHAPTER I.

Concerning Helen of Troy.

HELEN OF TROY, out of Suydam Queen, was a high-stepping mare, one of the best tandem leaders that ever sidled out for a turn, and she was killed by an overdose of the joy of life. Bimbo, the stable trainer, was to blame; but only in part. Going back to the true source of cause and effect, it was her genial owner, familiarly known as Kindly Crewe, who was at fault, because he had been away for three weeks and because the last thing he had said to Bimbo was "Keep your hands off Helen; I like her full of oats."

She had grown so full of oats in that short space of time that in trying to race them out of her system in the Lower Paddock, she took a header over the fence, breaking one slim ankle and her neck. It was small comfort to say that no horse had ever before done such a fool thing, and that if the mare had so little sense as to try to stop a twenty-mile pace in three yards rather than jump a four-barred barrier, she deserved her fate. No; there was no comfort whatever in putting the blame on Helen of Troy, darling of the stable and of her master's heart.

On the day that Kindly was to return Bimbo took a twenty-four-hour leave by assault. He told Mrs. Crewe that he would rather spend the rest of his life mucking out the stalls of the Grady Short Haul Trucking Corporation than be on the place when the master came back; and, as to performing the feat of actually breaking the news to him, why, he'd rather run at the fence the way Helen did and break his own bally neck.

Staring at Bimbo's corpulent figure, Mrs. Crewe did not smile; she trembled. She wished she, too, could run away, and then thought for one cowardly moment of sending a telegram which would catch Kindly as he came through town. Promptly she put the impulse behind her and fell back on love to help her through the ordeal with such effect that Crewe was to remember the soft, firm feel of her straining arms for the rest of his days with a sort of adoring wonder. It was not Mrs. Crewe but Kindly himself who spoke first after the blow of the news was struck, and then only to comfort:

"Buck up, Nelly girl. Don't take it so much to heart, my dear."

This was all he ever said in regard to the death of Helen of Troy. He braced his shoulders and went calmly about his business, but not his pleasure. In person, he was one of those young-old men whose spines have been ramrod trained in the saddle and on the box seat, and who paint their cheeks with the brush of the keen morning breezes of autumn. Florid, you might have called him; tousled of hair shot with gray, bulky, but with the kindliness which had nicknamed him radiating from his eyes and face in a benign and perpetual glow.

He and Nelly had no living children. He loved Nelly—and horses; she loved him.

Horses had been his sole pleasure, but with the tragic death of his adored mare the love of a lifetime seemed to shrivel within him, and let no man wonder. For a blue-ribbon tandem leader is a rare thing. Leaders can and have been made, but such are mediocre. Your true leader—a rhythm of lovely flesh, slender bone and taut nerves, that beats the signal of the slip of the rein and the caress of the tossed lash at a turn with an instinct sympathy which makes horse and master one heart, one pulse and one understanding love—is never made, but born.

Such had been Helen of Troy. Watch Kindly Crewe bringing his team along at a spanking trot, shoulders squared, arms out, whip at the salute and Helen in the lead. See the ripple and the spring of her glossy body, the red glow of her wide nostrils, the forward prick of her nervous ears and the wise flashing of her noble eye.

3

"B-r-r-r-u ! Ho, my pretty! Up with your knees!
Swing wide! Swing wide! See the people stare! Out you
go for the turn, girlie! Cluck! Cluck!"

Was that the song that was ringing in Kindly's ears,
making him deaf to all other calls? No harsh word
escaped him, and he uttered no breath of reproach
against Fate or Bimbo, and least of all against Helen of
Troy. He was still the kindliest of men, but it was cruel
to see the way he turned his back on the paddocks and
the stables and crueler still to watch the withering of his
youth. Golf! Bridge! How pitifully ineffectual were his
mind and hands, so adept at a grander game!

And that was not the worst of it. His cheeks grew
pouchy, his shoulders drooped and his big chest looked
as if it were beginning to cave in. He would start to go
somewhere and then stop, as though, after all, it were
not worth while. Even in town, in the executive offices
of F. S. & K. D. Crewe, his eyes would suddenly quit
work, but stay wide open, so that they gave his secretary
the creeps.

CHAPTER II.

Horse Flesh in the Rough.

MRS. CREWE was at her wits' ends to know what to do, for a mood is not like a single moment of sorrow. It is continuous, intangible, something that cannot be surrounded by two arms.

Bimbo had run away, leaving to her the whole burden of breaking the terrible news, and she had handled the crisis magnificently. Now he felt that it was his turn. He knew horses and he knew his master. He knew just what was the matter with Kindly and he knew the only cure. A man's love for a woman is one thing—an individual loyalty; his love for horses is quite another. Your true horseman may have a great affection for a special pet, but what he loves and reveres from deep down in his being is not a horse but horseflesh—horseflesh as a temple of noble qualities, of endearing foibles, of an astonishing capacity for understanding and cooperation, and alas, for going to the bad. Horses have all the great traits of man and a few of the mean ones; courage, strength, loyalty, fortitude, and a kick below the belt for an enemy. They are more knowable and scarcely less lovable than women. Comfort does not depend in any one of them, but in all. These things Bimbo knew thoroughly, however far short he might have fallen of expressing them in words.

He mooned about the stables, sat on the top rails of the Upper and Lower Paddocks and stood for hours watching the Crewe string put through their paces at the end of a longe or hitched to the drag or a sulky. If there was an answer to Kindly's trouble, and his own, it was nuzzling its oats, rollicking on the fallow turf or trotting up and down before his eyes, if only he had the shrewdness to see it. He did not deceive himself for a moment with the thought that he might go outside for something to take the place of Helen of Troy. He knew instinctively that though Kindly's cure lay in a horse, it would be hopeless to attempt to force his purse in order to salve his heart. Spontaneity, surprise, joy in possession of an undreamed treasure—all these must Bimbo wrest from the gods that his intuition might come to full fruition.

And here was horseflesh in plenty. He began at the bottom. The two colts and the filly came in for first consideration, but they were too young; they represented altogether too long a wait. He discarded them with a sigh, but finally. There was quite a class of two-year-olds. These he mulled over in his mind during long wakeful hours and then watched for as many more as they were paraded before him in every type of harness from the dishabille of a hackamore to silver tabs and patent-leather blinkers. But never once did his own hands itch to grasp the reins with adept touch and send a message quivering down the oldest telegraph line known to man. Then came the hacks, and last of all the coach horses.

Crewe's four-in-hand of dappled grays was famous on two sides of the Western Ocean. They had carried off more blues than any one combination of horses is entitled to, if the indoor sport of showing teams in harness is to endure. They formed a close corporation which was next door to a monopoly, and would have been cordially hated had they been the property of any man less beloved than Kindly. It was with this renowned team that he was scheduled to lead the coach parade through Central Park in a last effort to bring back the days when a coach and four had the right of way in the public's heart no less than on the road.

Bimbo watched them swinging by, hitched to the drag ballasted with every stable hand that could climb aboard. He knew these horses so well—every ripple and swell of their muscles; every shade of their color, in and out of sweat; every dapple, every hair! He knew their moods and their power, their infinitesimal failings and their transcendent perfections; he knew them as a mother knows her own young. Alas, he knew them so well that, though his eyes dimmed with pride at the staccato thunder of their passing, he did not ask himself even subconsciously if there was another such as Helen of Troy among them. They were not individuals; they were a team and gloried in the fact. Hence their extraordinary collection of decorations.

There remained only the waste—the outcasts of the stable, few in number, each marked by some bar sinister of ineradicable fault either in disposition or physical ensemble. These could not even be sold as from the Crewe string. They were doomed to be shipped away via the back door as soon as a nondescript auction offered the chance of an ignominious and unostentatious exit. Besides the Upper and Lower Paddocks, there was another inclosure, also a paddock, but never spoken of as such. It was called the pasture in a tone that made one think of cows. Here were penned the outcasts—the pariahs of the equine House of Crewe.

Bimbo climbed down from the perch from which he had been sampling the top of the cream in horse-flesh and walked with dragging feet and lowered head toward the pasture. He walked as one without hope, but dogged in duty. Long since, he had abandoned all thought of casually picking out a winner by the exercise of sheer perspicacity and had fallen back by an unperceived transition to the ancient formula of deduction through elimination. He would not thus have named the process going on in his mind as he scuffed heavily along on his way to look over the despicable remnants of a great stable; he would have called it simply, passing up no bets.

He reached the gate to the pasture, folded his arms on its top bar, settled his chin on them and stared with lackluster gaze at the small bunch of blemished horses which was gathered in a hollow some distance away. At that range the most expert buyer would have been at a loss to pick and choose among them, but Bimbo needed to go no nearer. The mere sight of pastern, gaskin or hock, withers or buttock, was enough for him to reconstruct an entire tragedy. It was as he had foreseen. No glimmer of hope came to light his eyes which were rapidly turning glassy with despair. As he was leaving the gate, however, a form, silhouetted against the evening sky on a near-by knoll, drew his attention only to throw him into a rage.

George Agnew Chamberlain

CHAPTER III.

Bimbo Sees a Great Light.

THE OBJECT of his wrath was a magnificent gelding, steel-gray in color and gloriously dappled with shadowy spots as big as the palm of Bimbo's hamlike hand. To visiting horsemen he was a thing of indescribable beauty until they heard his name, and then he turned ugly by association before their eyes. He was a rebel of the first water and of uncertain age, but surely no chicken. His splendid teeth, too freely shown, marked him as over four and under seven. His name was Highboy, and Bimbo hated him with a whole-hearted hatred.

Now, a word as to Highboy and how he had come unheralded and unpedigreed to the Crewe stables. The explanation lay in his color, dappled-gray, and in the fact that Kindly's scouts had orders to buy in every horse of that particular shade that came into the market, the only other qualifications being as to size and soundness of limb. It was specifically stipulated that temper was no bar; and, as it happens, Bimbo himself had been the joyful discoverer of Highboy at a sinister sale where no questions were asked or answered and prices were correspondingly low.

Kindly's theory was excellently conceived. His dappled-gray coaching team was the pride of his heart, and being subject to the ills of accident and age was constantly backed by a string of understudies. He was not particular as to the temper of these supers, because, up to the advent of Highboy, he had been confident that he could handle all the spirits one skin could hold when bottled at the near wheel of a heavy coach and surrounded on two other dimensions by well-trained old-stagers.

But Highboy had kicked the stuffings out of this theory in five crowded minutes, and incidentally eaten a hole in the neck of his side partner before the excited grooms, swallowing their terror at the voice of command, were able to cast him free of harness and bit.

Since that day the rebellious gelding had lived a life of ease, all the more maddening to the conquered because his stable manners were perfect. He was easy to handle, loved to be manicured, curried and brushed, and would eat apples gently off the palm of a child's hand. Nevertheless and notwithstanding, no one had mentioned harness to him again. There seemed to be a general and tacit acceptance that Highboy's expression on that subject had been peculiarly final. Life, human and otherwise, also equipment, were too valuable in Kindly's estimation to be cast beneath the active feet of an equine cyclone that had cost only three hundred dollars in cash to the highest bidder.

Bimbo had been so elated at the moment of purchase, had brought the horse home in such a transport of pride and had so bragged of the price at which his astuteness had secured the prize of a season, that that miserable three hundred dollars immediately became a festering thorn in the flesh. The old trainer would gladly have wiped out the sting of defeat with three thousand of his hard-earned dollars had there been any practical method of so doing. But the iron of the situation went still deeper. Three lots of remnants had gone to the obscure auction block since Highboy's advent, yet he remained in slothful possession of bed and board.

"No, Bimbo," Kindly had said on the three occasions, "I can't do it, questions or no questions. It's on account of his gentle ways, you see. It might turn out that he would win some woman's heart and then break her neck. We'll just have to keep him, and at least he's easy to look at."

Easy to look at! As if that made things any better! Now, in the moment of his deepest despair of finding a cure for his sorely wounded master, Bimbo stared at the beauty of Highboy, at his perked ears, broad fore-head, fearless eye, arched neck; at the glorious dapples that came and went under the flick of the sunlight; at the splendid bush of his sweeping tail and at the five straight lines of a perfect horse—four cannons and a level back. God help him, what a waste! Bimbo's eyes grew bloodshot with rage; his lips parted, he swore and from swearing sank to vituperation.

"Gelding! Bah! Lounge lizard! Mantel ornament! Father unknown; likewise mother! Good to look at as naked sin and rotten from the ground up! Parasite and blatherskite ! Eunuch!"

Highboy pitched on his forefeet, flaunted his tail, threw up his widespread heels, insulted Bimbo, and then tore off to the farther side of the pasture, where he began to trot up and down, neck arched, nose in, ears pointing forward, hoofs spurning the sod and plume streaming on the wind. The old trainers' face turned purple with a fresh access of rage; he spat violently on the ground and turned his back on the grand-stand performance. That night, his bulky frame feeling unusu-ally exhausted, he retired early, but not to sleep. The vision of Highboy persecuted him. How could anything so lovely be intrinsically so mean? Quite suddenly he came to a tremendous resolve. He would hitch High-boy to two tons of drag, with a board fence between him and the heaviest, staidest offwheeler in the stable, and either break him or kill him or be killed. His own life had so lost its savor that he risked only the small end of nothing. Who would choose to live on with his mouth full of ashes when he might go down gloriously in combat with a mortal enemy? The more he thought of the scheme the better it looked. Elimination of every other possibility had led him finally to Highboy. Anything which would change suddenly the status of the rebel must surely appeal to Kindly's dormant affection for horseflesh in the essence.

Here would be spontaneity, surprise and joy in possession of an undreamed treasure, all rolled into one! What if he, Bimbo, should fail and die in the attempt? Well, there were times when a lot can be said for death as a boon. What if he should kill Highboy? He produced a grin in the dark which was a cross between a sardonic grimace and a gleam of pure glee. His sane judgment told him that Kindly would consider the event an economic relief. He could hardly wait for the morning, and thus thinking he slept and slept soundly.

Now, many a man has gone to bed with a problem and awaked to find its answer staring him in the face. Thus with Bimbo. He thought he had hit on a daring attempt at solution of his trouble on the night before, but when he awoke an idea stood waiting for him which for sheer boldness made his previous scheme seem faint-hearted cowardice.

It was as though the apparition of Highboy had been in reality an important message, an attempt at long-distance horse telegraphy, a hunch in the making, which had knocked and knocked in vain on the barred door of Bimbo's waking intelligence and then given up the struggle only to creep into the warm emptiness of his sleeping brain and fill the vacant apartment chockablock with its presence.

He did not stop to reason. He clambered out of bed and into his clothes by six of the clock, Eastern standard time. By seven Highboy was in his stall; by 7:30 he had munched two quarts of oats and by eight he was reveling beneath such a combing and rubbing down as had not been his portion in many weeks. By 8:30 he was in harness and by 8:35 Bimbo was beating it for the manor house as fast as his stumpy legs and stumpier breath would permit him to travel. He actually had the pleasurable illusion that he was flying. He burst into the morning room where Kindly, alone, was dejectedly eating a leisurely breakfast preparatory to catching the 9:05 for town.

CHAPTER IV.

Fired for Five Minutes.

THE FACIAL contortions induced by the emotions of disaster or great joy are astoundingly similar; consequently, and since Bimbo remained for a moment speechless by force of circumstances and the weight of his paunch, it was natural that Kindly should have picked the wrong answer to his trainer's inarticulate commotion and spoken as follows:

"If anything has happened to one of the horses, Bimbo, just shoot him and put him out of his misery. If it's anything else, use your own judgment. Whatever it is, don't bother me."

"I won't bother you, Mr. Crewe," said Bimbo, recovering his breath, "further than to request you to walk as far as the Upper Paddock." Ordinarily the trainer addressed his employers as Kindly, except when before strangers or in the show ring, and the extremely formal opening of the interview should have warned Crewe that something unusual was afoot, something so formidable that it could not be carelessly brushed aside. His eyes assumed the vacant stare that on several recent occasions had proved so disconcerting to his secretary. With a shrug of his shoulders which looked more like a shrinking quiver, he turned on Bimbo.

"Get this straight," he said; "I'm not going near the paddocks, and, what's more, I'm not going to drive in the coach parade."

"Not—going—to—drive—in—the—coach—parade!" whispered Bimbo with a pause between each word, his eyes slowly bulging from his head.

"That's what I said," confirmed Kindly. His eyes grew vacant again. "I'm still trying to decide," he continued presently, "whether I'll show this year at all."

"Trying—trying to decide whether you'll show!" gulped Bimbo, amazement in his florid face and tears in his voice. Then suddenly he awoke from the trance into which his master's terrible words had plunged him. His bulldog chin shot out and his head up. "Listen to me!" he roared. "I've spoken to you as trainer to his boss and you wouldn't hear. Now it's Bimbo to Kindly and man to man. Listen to me! You're going to the Upper Paddock if I have to call the hands and carry you there. You're going now! Do you get that?"

"I heard you," said Kindly quietly. "You're fired, of course, Bimbo. I'm sorry."

"Fired!" snorted Bimbo. "Well, I don't care a damn if I am! Who minds being fired for five minutes? Will you come or do you still want to make it a ride?"

Kindly's eyes grew hard for the first time in the twelve happy years of almost brotherly companionship with his trainer. They became two points of steel which drilled Bimbo through and through. It was a look which in any other moment would have struck terror to his lion heart, but in this instance he took it so calmly that a shadow of doubt swept across Kindly's troubled face. But only for an instant. He drew out his watch.

"I'll come," he said shortly, "just for the five minutes it will take me to put Charlie in charge."

Side by side, and in silence, the two estranged friends, comrades in many a shared victory, left the house and walked briskly toward the stables; but with a difference. Kindly carried his head low, while Bimbo seemed to be striving to stretch his short neck to the heavens. His eyes protruded like the orbs of a crab as they strained forward for a first sight of the distant paddock, and were filled with a reaching anxiety which changed suddenly to complacent joy. His heart began to pound with something more than the labor of mere physical exertion.

"Hold it, boy!" he murmured inaudibly in exalted supplication. "Hold it, my beauty!"

The path to the stables led the two men close to the great Upper Paddock, which embraced the four-furlong practice track. As they approached the fence, Bimbo, in spite of himself, slanted stealthly eyes at Kindly; and Kindly, knowing that he was watched, kept his gaze stubbornly on the ground. The consequence was that Kindly saw where he was going and Bimbo did not; Kindly stepped over a hose, while Bimbo tripped on it and all but came a purler. As he rushed headlong to catch up with his balance Kindly shot one glance across the fence and forthwith came violently to a stop.

The sight which met his eyes was the eighth, ninth and tenth wonder of the world. On the fresh green turf, well away from the track, stood the high English dogcart, two idle grooms and two horses, hitched tandem. The wheeler, a splendid bay, tried and true, was a bit restive from the chest up, tossing his head impatiently; but the leader, steel gray and darkly dappled, seemed posed in weathered Pentelic marble. From the straight-hanging plume of his tail, along the sheer line of his level back, over the curve of his arched neck and up to and including his erect ears, he was as fixed as a painting—only he lived. Waves of electric life throbbed from his still body to beat against Kindly's bursting temples.

"What horse is that?" he asked sharply.

"Highboy, sir," replied Bimbo promptly, without pausing to wonder at the question.

"How long has he stood like that?" continued Kindly, laying trembling hands on the top rail of the fence to steady himself.

"Since I told him to hold it while I fetched you," answered Bimbo out of the fullness of his faith. He sidled up to Kindly and suddenly all his pent emotions came burbling out in a volley of chatter: "Great balls of sweat, Kindly, don't you tumble? Don't you know he knows you're looking at him? Pride, by God! He's in the lead, ain't he? He's out and free; he's alone, not one of a level bunch. He's It, and he knows it just like you and me when we're on the box with the horn tallyhoing to make the people stare."

"You're right, Bimbo," gulped Kindly.

He was still in a daze; he was choking; he was at the very bottom of a translucent sea and he would drown if he didn't get to the top in a hurry. Up he came, and up. His shoulders began to straighten and his chest to bulge. All the blood in his veins started to race from his heels to his head. It was like the sap of springtime, hurrying back with youth to a stricken world. It lifted him, bore him swiftly upward until he shot out of the deep waters into the freedom of a new air.

"You're right," he breathed exultantly, staring hungrily at Highboy.

21

George Agnew Chamberlain

CHAPTER V.

Harmony in Harness.

AS THOUGH Kindly had called, the some-
time rebel turned his head with a slow, majestic
movement and looked his owner square in the eyes.
Instantly Kindly's body became vibrant. He slipped
over the fence as smoothly as a snake over a stone wall,
approached the horse quietly, and reaching out a steady
hand began to caress him. Lowering his nose, Highboy
promptly butted him in the chest and struck the sod a
single sharp blow with his right fore hoof.

"I get you!" cried Kindly with boyish jubilation as
he recoiled from the dignified and firm rebuff. "You
mean 'Let's go!'"

He started toward the cart wheel, his arms extended
and his fingers working as though they were in rehearsal
for a half-forgotten play. The grooms moved forward,
stood at attention and laid strong hands on the reins
close to the bits. The horses quivered and pawed; bent

their heads and cast them up again, almost lifting the grooms from their feet. Kindly sprang smoothly to the driver's box with a catlike alacrity astonishing in one of his generous build and recent age. He picked up the rug, wrapped it around his thighs in knowing manner, sank back on the high pad, leaned forward, gathered the lines and lifted the whip from the socket.

"Cast loose, boys," he said quietly, "and stand free."

The grooms complied and leaped aside; the horses shot forward on a bee line across the sward, moving in a swift but nervous, jerky trot. For a moment they pulled hard, tightening the wires, listening, ears back, for a message, and presently it came to them. It told of gentle, knowing hands giving them their will for a moment—velvet in the mouth for a moment—and then whispering steadily of the strength of steel. For that they had waited—the touch and call of the master. They heard and answered, eased their weight from the bits, pricked their ears forward and steadied down, freeing themselves from domination by obedience to the law. They became a glorious rhythm, a harmony, smooth to the eye, melodious to the ear.

They were making at right angles for the track and the fence, but Kindly had no intention of risking an expert turn. He bore down gently on the left reins as if he were guiding a commonplace bobsled. Gradually he brought the team around in a wide sweep to the track; and then, bit by bit, moment by moment, gave them their heads until they were racing along at a thunderous trot. Around they went and around once more. He eased them, let them go, eased them again, talking soft words to Highboy, getting acquainted, telling him confidential things in a low tone which suggested further intimacies and perhaps love in the near future.

As they passed for the second time the gaping stable crowd which had gathered around Bimbo, Kindly called out in a clear voice, "Open the gate!"

"No, Kindly," protested Bimbo. "Not today!"

His shout floated down the wind, weakening into a wail as he saw his master swing from the track to the turf and, with slip of rein and touch of lash, boldly venture on a broad figure eight. At the first turn Highboy seemed to check and waver, but in reality his lithe body was merely squirming to get a message and get it quickly—and it came.

"B-r-r-u !" Kindly caught up a six-inch loop over the middle knuckle of his driving hand. "Cluck! Cluck!" He let the loop go and at the same instant cast the whip's lash gently to Highboy's off shoulder. Into his full stride swung the gelding, leaning for the left swerve. Swiftly they made the small circle. "B-r-r-u !" again, slip of rein, lash to the other shoulder, "Cluck! Cluck!" and an all but perfect turn to the right. They came out of the figure eight and straightened. Bimbo forced back the gate with his own hands to give them the joy of the open road and the freedom of the wide world.

An hour later Kindly, perched on a stool, and Bimbo on a feed box, were assisting at Highboy's toilet after exercise. No words can describe the affection and admiration, amounting almost to awe, with which they regarded him. Kindly was still bubbling over with the feats of intelligence and intuition which the horse had performed during the morning's work-out and related them seriatim and over and over to his avid audience of one. But these wonders of technic faded into nothingness beneath the shadow of the great miracle of Highboy himself—Highboy as the triumphant vindication of horseflesh as an essence, one and indivisible.

"You may be thinking, Bimbo," said Kindly, "that he's been a leader before, away back somewhere in his stormy past; but I tell you he hasn't. I know it! I don't mean to say he jackknifed on me. No; nothing so crude as that; but he asked questions all the time!"

"Did he now?" exclaimed Bimbo, even while he nodded his head up and down to indicate that he could quite understand the marvel. Half an hour later Kindly was still talking.

"I ask you, Bimbo," he was saying portentously, "what's behind all this business of coach and four, high cart, sulky or any bit of clean-stepping prettiness between the shafts? Why do we do it? Horse and man, why do we love it? I'll tell you. Just two things—exhilaration and admiration. Take one away and the other is spoiled. And don't forget the horses are in on both. You bet they are ! They drain the joy from action and the nectar from the public eye. Look at Highboy here! Golly! See the coxcomb turn his head! What happened to him this morning? No; I don't want you to talk. I'll tell you. The same thing as has put many a pretty woman over the hurdles. Boredom and vanity in conjunction with the psychological moment."

"Sure-lee!" interjected Bimbo, spitting at a grain of oats and hitting it. "That's what he fell for!"

"Don't think I'm not giving you credit, Bimbo," resumed Kindly hurriedly. "I am, and your pay's raised 10 per cent from this day. Now, here's what I was saying, only clearer: The horse is the thing, of course; but what makes him show is the public eye, just the same as you and me when we're on the box with four reins in one hand and the whip at the salute. Do you get me, Bimbo? What I mean is, when there's no one left to cry 'Oh, look! Look!' as we come bowling along, and all we hear is 'Gee! See what's got away from Buffalo Bill!' why, coaching will be finished, metaled roads or no metaled roads."

Bimbo shook his head affirmatively. "When you or me is on the box of a sharpish morning, Kindly, we be just kids—and the horses too." "That's it," confirmed

Kindly, rising from the stool to flex his muscles. He opened and bent his arms with a snap; his eyes sparkled and his face radiated such joy that it seemed to illumine the stable with a golden light. He threw back his head and drew a long breath. Ye gods, what smells! Pungent oats and hay. Warm odors, more vulgar. The acrid smell of sweat and the sweet breath of horses. Leather—leather, bright, and new; leather, worn and dry; leather, polished to the flower of old oak! Then his eyes fell upon Highboy and promptly filled with the illuminating moisture which is the visual distillation of happiness. He went to the horse, cast his right arm over his withers, pressed against him, caressed him. This time he was not repulsed. Highboy spoke to him with a whimpering whinny, curved his neck sharply and rubbed with his nose first Kindly's empty pocket and then his dangling and equally empty left hand.

"Heigh! Someone fetch me an apple, and fetch it quick!" called Kindly as his fingers crept along the bulging muscle beneath the mane and sought the two hollows behind the pointed ears. "What a hide, Bimbo! Baby's skin, here behind the ears of him. Not a blemish anywhere. All dappled silk, from eyes to buttocks. What a glory of a horse to be reborn, all in a morning, from a bit of understanding flattery!"

When Kindly finally wandered back to the house along toward one o'clock, still smiling from the depths of a happy daze, his wife greeted him with the following words:

"Why, Kindly Crewe! Did you miss your train? What on earth are you doing here? You know I never eat anything myself for lunch." And then as she really looked at him, "Oh, my dear, what has happened? Whatever it is I am glad!"

At the end of a week the office, which had been worrying itself sick over his sad and too continual presence, began to howl over his absence, as is the way of offices, and to predict dire results if he did not come to town by the first train or a flying machine. It pointed out that his many previous absences had been premeditated and consequently predigested by the monster organization, but this was different. There were deals to be closed; checks to be signed; papers, documents, that awaited his decision.

In the meantime—see Kindly and his tandem team seeking out the widest of the clay roads in the oak-and-pine belt. The oaks have turned; their leaves are red as pigeon's blood against the dark and juicy green of the everlasting pines. The air tingles and tinkles with the first prickings of the frost. Look at Kindly, the youth of him! Shoulders squared, arms out, whip at the salute and Highboy in the lead. Up—up into the collar for the open stretch. Oh, the beauty of his action, the pride of his head, the joy and the spring and the drive of his stride! "I'm Highboy! Highboy! King of the road for a day!" And then—

"B-r-r-r-u ! Ho, my beauty! Up with your knees! Swing wide! Swing wide! Pipe the guy that's standing there to watch you take the turn! Cluck! Cluck!"

No slip of rein, no expert tossing of the guiding lash, for Highboy knows it all and more. Out he sidles, leans for the turn and flashes into line again, trotting free and wide, crash for crash with the hoof beats of the bay between the shafts. On they go, sailing along on whirling pin wheels of brilliant red, tempted to nick the outer edge of the foolish town—tempted and yielding. Not the thick of the traffic. Oh, no! Just into the park and out again, to see the people stare!

Before Bimbo could scratch his ear, so to speak, show week was upon them and the Crewe string entered for a try at every class. Kindly drove, Bimbo drove, and Charlie, the head groom, nervously took his turn. They showed everything that wears leather for pleasure and in due course worked down to "Hackneys; tandem." Long had been the debate waged between Kindly and Bimbo and back again as to just what Highboy would do in the ring and whether they should show him at all, always to come up against the blank wall of the question, "What if the judges call for a canter?"

Now a word as to cantering tandem, trickiest of all equine maneuvers, barring the *haute ecole*. The driver takes his team on the trot, straight at a solid barrier. At the very moment of the right-angled swerve the horses must change lead and break into a canter; but that is not all. Just one thing more: Leader and wheeler must start in step, hoof for hoof and stride for stride. The real question—the silent question behind all the spoken ones asked by Kindly of Bimbo and by Bimbo of Kindly was, "Can living man throw Highboy into a canter and bring him out again short of the Canadian border?"

"Well," concluded Kindly, "perhaps the judges won't call for it. They don't have to, and they haven't for three seasons on end. And what if they do? Perhaps Highboy will go through it once, just to show off. Anyway, I'm not going to try him out—not once; not even here in the paddock. If he killed himself or me before I trot him up and down under the noses of the boys who thought they had a laugh on you, Bimbo, why, I'd never forgive myself—never!"

The great day and the fateful hour came. There were five tandem teams and Kindly drove fourth. If the quantity and quality of the rattle of applause which followed the evolutions of the pedigreed bay and the brilliant dappled gray of unknown lineage meant anything to the judges, it surely meant another blue ribbon to the Crewe stables. Highly pleased with the world in general, himself and Highboy in particular, Kindly stepped briskly from the ring, looked at his watch and saw he must hurry to dress in time for dinner.

Friends stopped him right and left, some for a hasty word and some for the outline of the horse in history. They knew it was not in him to be brusque, and, one and all, they never missed a chance to take a leisurely warm bath in his smile whenever opportunity offered. Consequently, by the time he reached the outer lobby the best part of half an hour had passed, and as he stood there for one last handshake there came rolling out to him an uproar shot through with jabs of lightning in the shape of shouts of "Kindly! Kindly!"

Opening a way for himself with a plowing shoulder, he rushed back to the ring and for a single second stood transfixed. In the center of the tanbark was his best English dogcart with Bimbo on the drivers' seat. In front of Bimbo was the wheeler, quivering but steady, and in front of the wheeler stood Highboy, erect on his hind legs and looking as high as the Woolworth Building as he thrashed around with his forefeet and madly tried to throw bit and bridle from his tossing head.

"So," raced the thought through Kindly's brain, "the judges called them back for a canter, after all, and Bimbo couldn't find me!"

He tore off hat and coat as he leaped into the ring, and in a moment was slipping up over one wheel of the cart as Bimbo, trembling and purple with rage, surrendered the reins and descended via the other.

"B-r-r-r-u! You dappled devil!" shouted Kindly.

Down came Highboy to all fours, deliberately turned his head all the way round and looked at his friend and master as one who would say, "So you're back where you belong, are you?"

Under cover of the ecstatic roar from the crowd, Kindly leaned over and spoke to the spluttering Bimbo:

"Oh, never mind that! I know what happened. They've called for a canter. Tell me quick, has he seen any of the other teams do it?"

"Three," answered Bimbo—"all rotten."

The bugle sounded. Kindly telegraphed a message along the tautened lines. The team sprang forward in unison and he began to talk aloud.

"Up with your knees, boy! Into your collar! Snap into it! Show them—show them how! Now! Hoop-la, Highboy! You've got it! Hold it! Hold it! Steady boy! Whoa!"

The grooms sprang to the horses' heads. As he helped his master down, Bimbo chortled in a raucous voice, all malice forgotten, "What a canter, eh, Mr. Crewe? Oh, you, Highboy!"

"The top of the cream, Bimbo!" answered Kindly, blinking the tears from his shining eyes. "Smooth as music and moonlight. I didn't do anything. Really, I didn't. He did it all himself. He isn't a horse at all. He's something God thought of just once."

"Well," murmured Bimbo reflectively, "I wouldn't lay quite the whole of it on God. If you'd heard some of the things I called him while he stood on his hind legs for five solid minutes, trying to paw holes in the roof, perhaps you'd get my meaning."

"Why, that's the very thing I was thinking of!" laughed Kindly with upthrown head. "He was made just for himself and me."

CHAPTER VI.

The Curtain Falls.

TWO WEEKS later Kindly and his blue-ribbon team were back on the soft roads of the open country. The parchment leaves of the oaks were hanging on through the grim, cold winds of winter and the pines loomed big and dark above the bare, brown soil. But life ran with a surging note, high and full, through the veins of horse and man. They were coming in from a ten-mile tearing drive, and as of old the lure of town and people was strong upon them. Just a nick into the town, dash across the Boulevard, into the park and out again! This was the song of hoof and heart: "Rat-tat, tat-tat! Here we come! Look! Look! Aren't we lovely! Aren't we strong? And young, young, young!"

As they swept up to a crossing at a spanking trot, Kindly saw grouped on the left curb a shrimp of a man pushing a loaded baby carriage, and behind him his wife and two children of walking size. On the right was a narrow walk and the pronged iron fence of a great estate. To Kindly and the rushing horses it mattered not that the family group was greasy to look at and bundled in garments that poisoned the winter air. They were people—people with eyes to see, ears to hear and hearts to leap in admiration.

Suddenly an icy chill shot through Kindly's extended arms. The man saw them, and yet he had started to cross with the woman and children strung out behind him! What on earth were they thinking? Didn't they know? Gangway! Gangway! Did they take a tandem in flying-wedge formation for a motor car with horn, emergency brake and clapperty chains that could stop in its own length? In the terror of that instant Kindly grew hard, and rage seized him as he yelled at the top of his voice, "Heigh! You! Look out!"

He saw the man's face turn and leer at him with sneering lip as he kept on straight into the path of the flying team. Kindly's hands ate up the reins for a short hold. He knew he could lift Highboy, but never the wheeler. A baby, God help him! He could almost have killed the man with joy; but a baby! He had the lines at last wrapped to his elbows. He braced his feet, bent his back forward to the coming strain, but never needed to pull. Highboy waited for no order; he shot straight into the air, leaped high, twisted violently to the side and fell, impaled to the heart on the sharp prongs of the iron fence. Wheeler and cart wrenched around to follow and crashed against his hanging buttocks, already quivering in the death throe. Kindly was hurled over and through the wreckage to find himself standing on numbed feet directly above the baby carriage and the rat-faced little man.

"Are you *crazy?*" he choked.

"*You* crazy," replied the stranger with alien accent, and walked on, uncurious, his family trailing stolidly behind him.

Late that night, when Bimbo came to the manor house to report that all that could be done in the way of cleaning up the pitiful mess had been accomplished, he found word that Kindly wished to see him in person, and followed the maid to the library with quaking heart. He expected to find his master an utterly broken man, but apparently Kindly had more than recovered from the actual shock of the disaster. Instead of breaking, it seemed rather to have added something to him. He was reading a book as Bimbo entered, and the eyes he raised from its pages were calm and warmly affectionate.

"Sit down, Bimbo," he said. "This isn't a business interview, though I may tell you of some radical changes in the classes of horses we are to breed from now on. What I want to do tonight is to talk about Highboy. I want to fix him for all time in my mind just as he was— the oneness and the pride of him—and I'll tell you why.

He taught me something. That isn't it, either. He gave me something—something besides his life, I mean."

Bimbo nodded his bullet head solemnly and started to speak, but Kindly stopped him with a raised hand and continued: "You know, they say the heart can't remember for long the features of a face. Try to think of someone you've loved who is gone, and what do you remember? Some favorite photograph of that face and perhaps where it was taken. But Highboy didn't have features; he had points. A warm eye on a broad forehead. Let's remember that. Winged nostrils and a chest like an apron of silk. Clean forelegs that he could use like a boxer. Dapples! What dapples, Bimbo; big as your hand, each with the luster of a black pearl behind a silvery veil! A strong hide and in it himself, courage and rebellion, docility and rage, an unconquerable spirit—undying flame!"

Bimbo's eyes became suffused.

"Let up on that, Kindly," he said gruffly and in haste. "I just been burying of him."

"So you have," said Kindly, untroubled but with understanding. "Well, old friend, this is what I wanted to tell you: The ratty little man with the baby carriage was right. If only you could have seen his face when he said '*You* crazy!' I am crazy; that is, I was crazy this morning. Don't eight million hooters blare the swan song I wouldn't hear? Haven't the metaled roads been tolling the death knell on us for a dozen years? And this is what Highboy did for me, Bimbo. He took the sting out of it. What a message! What a clarion call! What a sunset to our day of glory! God help us, Bimbo, what a curtain!"

COLOPHON.

The text is set in 12-point Baskerville Old Face, except for italics, which is 12-point Baskerville. Pagination does not follow the original edition.

The mission of the South Jersey Culture & History Center is to help foster awareness of the rich cultural and historical heritage of southern New Jersey, to promote the study of this heritage, especially among area students, and to produce publishable materials that provide lasting and deepened understanding of this heritage.

OTHER LITERARY TITLES
PUBLISHED BY SJCHC.

Dallas Lore Sharp. *Seasons.*
"Nature appears at her best when Dallas Lore Sharp introduces it." So wrote an anonymous book reviewer in the *Journal of Education* in August 1912 about the author of *Seasons.* Born in 1870 in Haleyville, New Jersey, Sharp spent his childhood roaming the woods beside the Cohansey and Maurice Rivers, and went on to become one of the most popular nature writers of his day. A "rare and honest soul," he sought to inspire young people to share his appreciation for the glories of the natural world, available in their own backyards. *Seasons* presents a selection of essays first published in Sharp's *The Whole Year Round.* 158 pages, paperback.
ISBN: 978-0-9888731-1-7. $14.95

Dallas Lore Sharp. *The Nature of Things.*
Our second volume of engaging nature essays from Sharp's *The Whole Year Round* (originally published in 1915). Dallas Lore Sharp, born in 1870 in Haleyville, Cumberland County, New Jersey, was an outstanding essayist writing for young adults in the early twentieth century.
179 pages, paperback.
ISBN: 978-1-947889-00-2. $14.95

Samuel Scoville Jr. *Everyday Adventures.*

Twelve essays that describe Samuel Scoville Jr.'s jaunts into nature with arresting detail and introduce readers to hibernating mammals, snakes, orchids, and other flora, but especially to birds. Whether listening to birdsong, searching for hidden nests (which remain undisturbed), or quietly observing avian daily routines, Scoville describes his surroundings vividly and often with considerable wit. He recounts expeditions in Connecticut, the Berkshires, Pennsylvania, Delaware, the Pine Barrens, and the far north of Canada. Quickly, readers find that they have stepped into everyday adventures of their own.

252 pages, paperback.

ISBN: 978-0-9976699-9-2. $14.95

Samuel Scoville Jr. *The Out of Doors Club.*

A collection of essays that follows the adventures of the "Band," a group of young siblings led on imagination-filled hikes by their father. In twenty brief essays, many set in the Pine Barrens, Samuel Scoville Jr. reminds readers of simpler times, when the world held fewer cares and nature walks with a parent could be the highlight of a day. Trekking through fields, bogs and forests, canoing down rivers, the Band learn amusing lessons about nature and life. Readers will appreciate the gentle and loving relationship depicted between father, mother and children.

147 pages, paperback.

ISBN: 978-1-947889-90-3. $14.95

Charles K. Landis. *A Trip to Mars.*

Charles K. Landis, prominent real estate developer and founder of Vineland and Sea Isle City, wrote this foray into science fiction on an early typewriter c. 1876. The title alternates between thrilling storytelling and thinly veiled commentary on the social

ills of Earth. A pair of intrepid travelers journey to Mars, explore its geography, confront terrifying monsters, and encounter the ancient culture and philosophy of the Martians, from whom the Earthlings may learn much. Never before published. With an introduction by Patricia Martinelli.
136 pages, paperback.
ISBN: 978-0-9888731-5-5. $14.95

Gary B. Giberson. *Swan Bay Jim & Gasoline Seventeen Cents a Gallon; Moonshine a Dollar a Quart.*
The mayor of Port Republic for over three decades, Gary B. Giberson is a master decoy-carver, entrepreneur, and author. This volume pairs two short stories with illustrations from distinguished artist Kathy Anne English. Follow a poignant hunt through the cedar swamps of the Mullica River and join an adventurous chase to capture rum runners during Prohibition.
40 pages, paperback.
ISBN: 978-0-9976699-4-7. $5.00

www.ingramcontent.com/pod-product-compliance
Lightning Source LLC
Jackson TN
JSHW011512260125
77712JS00015B/236